SUPER BOWL
NEW ENGLAND PATRIOTS
CHAMPIONS

Published by Creative Education
123 South Broad Street
Mankato, Minnesota 56001
Creative Education is an imprint of The Creative Company.

DESIGN AND PRODUCTION BY **EVANSDAY DESIGN**

LIBRARY OF CONGRESS CATALOGING-IN-PUBLICATION DATA

LeBoutillier, Nate.
New England Patriots / by Nate LeBoutillier.
p. cm. — (Super Bowl champions)
Includes index.
ISBN 1-58341-386-3
1. New England Patriots (Football team)—Juvenile literature. I. Title. II. Series.
GV956.N36L43 2005
796.332'64'0974461—dc22   2005048365

First edition

9 8 7 6 5 4 3 2 1

COVER PHOTO: running back Corey Dillon

PHOTOGRAPHS BY
AP/Wide World Photos, Corbis (Bettmann, Reuters), Getty Images (Elsa, JEFF HAYNES/AFP, MARK LEFFINGWELL/AFP, JOHN MOTTERN/AFP, Ezra Shaw),
SportsChrome USA

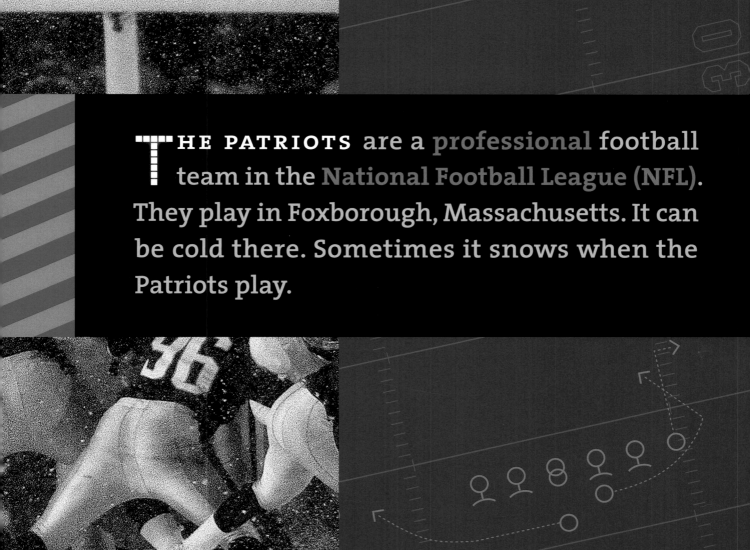

THE PATRIOTS are a professional football team in the National Football League (NFL). They play in Foxborough, Massachusetts. It can be cold there. Sometimes it snows when the Patriots play.

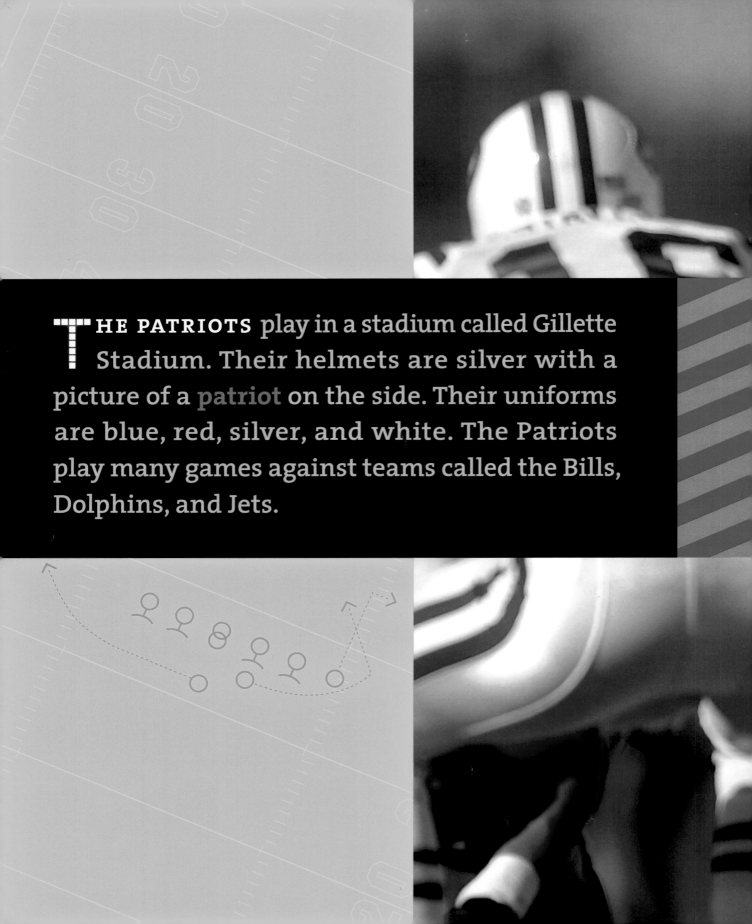

THE PATRIOTS play in a stadium called Gillette Stadium. Their helmets are silver with a picture of a patriot on the side. Their uniforms are blue, red, silver, and white. The Patriots play many games against teams called the Bills, Dolphins, and Jets.

The Patriots changed their uniforms and helmets in 1993.

The Boston Patriots won a lot of games in the 1960s ^

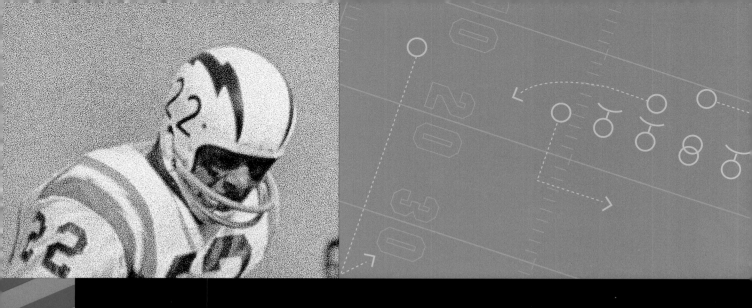

BOSTON, MASSACHUSETTS, was the Patriots' first home. They played there for 10 seasons. The Boston Patriots played in a championship game in 1963. But they lost to the San Diego Chargers 51–10.

STEVE GROGAN played quarterback for the Patriots. He was tough and played even when he was hurt. In 1985, he helped the Patriots get to their first Super Bowl. But they lost to the Chicago Bears 46–10.

DREW BLEDSOE was a good quarterback, too. He could throw the ball hard and far. He helped the Patriots get to the Super Bowl in 1996. But they lost again. Fans thought the Patriots would never win the big game.

IN 2001, Drew Bledsoe got hurt. Tom Brady took his place and helped the Patriots get to the Super Bowl. The Patriots upset the St. Louis Rams on a last-second kick to win the game. Patriots fans finally cheered for a championship!

Tom Brady's passes usually landed right on target.

The Patriots had many smart and fast players on defense ^

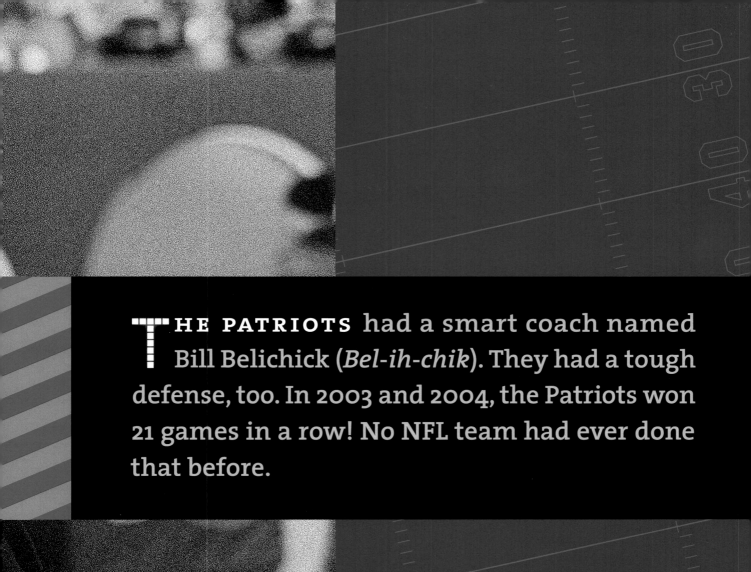

THE PATRIOTS had a smart coach named Bill Belichick (*Bel-ih-chik*). They had a tough defense, too. In 2003 and 2004, the Patriots won 21 games in a row! No NFL team had ever done that before.

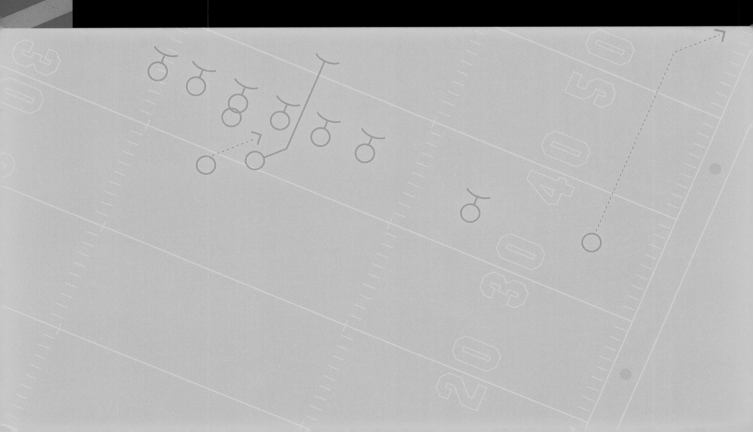

THE PATRIOTS won two more Super Bowls in 2003 and 2004. First they beat the Carolina Panthers in an exciting game. Then they beat the Philadelphia Eagles to win their third world championship.

TODAY, THE Patriots are the best team in the NFL. Patriots fans hope that Coach Belichick and Tom Brady will help the team win more Super Bowls!

National Football League (NFL)
a group of football teams that play against each other;
there are 32 teams in the NFL today

patriot
one of the first soldiers in the United States

professional
a person or team that gets paid to play or work

upset
when a team that is not expected to win beats
the other team

FUN FACTS

Team colors
Blue, red, silver, and white

Home stadium
Gillette Stadium (68,436 seats)

Conference/Division
American Football Conference (AFC), East Division

First season
1960

Super Bowl wins
2001 (beat St. Louis Rams 20–17)
2003 (beat Carolina Panthers 32–29)
2004 (beat Philadelphia Eagles 24–21)

Training camp location
Foxborough, Massachusetts

NFL Web site for kids
http://www.playfootball.com